Let's Dance

By Julie Haydon

Illustrations by Stevie Mahardhika

T0342750

Contents

How to Create a Dance

Goal

To create and perform a dance.

Materials

- dancers
- a selection of music to choose from
- a music player
- paper
- a pen
- a rehearsal space
- a large mirror
- clothing and material for costumes
- props
- make-up
- a performance space
- an audience

3

Steps

Creating the dance

1. Decide how many dancers will perform the dance.

2. Listen to several pieces of music and choose one to dance to.

3. Play the music again and write down how the music makes everyone feel.

4. Decide if the dance is going to tell a story or just be a series of movements with a theme.

5. Start creating the movements. Include a variety of dance steps, as well as fast and slow movements and movements at different heights. Play the music if this helps.

6. Write down the movements and make sure they will work well in the performance space.

Preparing the dance

7. Do a warm-up.

8. Practise the movements in front of a mirror with the music playing. Show emotion with your faces and bodies.

9. Choose costumes that suit the dance but are also easy to dance in.

10. Decide on any props the dance needs. Keep the props simple.

11. Rehearse the dance together until everyone knows the routine.

12. Invite friends and family to watch the dance.

Performing the dance

13. Set up the performance space and put the props in place.

14. Put on costumes and make-up, and style hair.

15. Prepare for the dance by doing a warm-up.

16. When the audience is seated, start the music.

17. Perform the dance.

18. Bow to the audience at the end of the performance.

Swan Lake

Last night, I attended a performance of the classical ballet Swan Lake. This ballet was created more than 100 years ago. The choreography was by Marius Petipa and Lev Ivanov, and the music was written by Peter Tchaikovsky.

Swan Lake is about a young woman, Odette, who is under a spell cast by the evil magician Rothbart. This spell turns her into a white swan during the day. She is human only between midnight and dawn. A prince, Siegfried, promises to love and marry her. If he stays true to his word, Odette will be free.

Nelson Promotions presents
Swan Lake
at the Concert Hall
7.30 pm 30 August
Stalls   Row K   Seat 4

Prince Siegfried and Odette dance in front of the swans.

However, Rothbart and his daughter, Odile, trick Siegfried into vowing his love for Odile. When Siegfried realises his mistake, he rushes to Odette. They jump into a lake together and drown, and Rothbart's power is destroyed.

Rothbart and Odile

Swan Lake was the first ballet I'd seen and I enjoyed it very much. The dancers were strong and graceful. I was amazed at how high the dancers could leap and how fast they could turn around and around on one foot.

The women wore special ballet shoes so they could dance on their toes. It's called dancing "en pointe". When they danced en pointe, they looked almost as light as feathers.

The parts of Odette and Odile were danced by the same ballerina. As Odette, she wore white and was graceful and shy. As Odile, she wore black and was confident and bold.

Odette

Odile

My favourite part was when four ballerinas, who were dressed as little white swans, danced together in a line. They held hands across the front of their bodies and moved at exactly the same time.

I loved the dramatic music and the costumes were beautiful. The way the backdrops and the simple props changed was clever and it helped to set the scene on stage.

In the future I want to see other ballets, including different versions of Swan Lake.